WILLOW .....And THE MEDUSA

Other Books by this Author

Enlisted at 14......A Memoir

Enlisted at 14......And the Journey Continues

Willow...A Novel

Just a Dream

For: Craven Stone Sr.

CHAPTER 1

Jesse awoke when he felt something stick him in his back, a mosquito he thought. Then it happened again, that's a hell of a big mosquito he recalls, there it was again, about the same spot. He was lying on his stomach so he raised his right hand to feel where he was bit but when he rubbed his shoulder it felt wet. When he brought his hand around to see what it was he saw that it was blood. What the hell he said, then he notice the girl he had stayed with that night with a penknife standing over him sticking him in the back. The blade dripping blood, his blood. Hey bitch, what the fuck you doing? He immediately slapped the knife out of her hand and went upside her head. Just *what in the hell do you think you doing he said*

again?

She started crying telling Jesse that she heard word that he was screwing someone else and she got to laying there thinking about it, couldn't sleep and felt she didn't want anyone screwing him but her. I couldn't take it, I'm sorry, I'm really sorry Jesse.

Damn that!

You ever thought about waking me up and us talking about this shit? No, the first thing you do is stick a blade in my Damn back, what kind of shit is that? And you know you were my main squeeze. Jesse I'm sorry, I'm going to make it right for you let me go into the bathroom and get the medical kit. When she left out the room Jesse jumped up grab his shoes without putting them on and headed for the door. I'm getting the fuck out of here, I don't know what she going to come back with next, 357 Mag maybe. When he reached the door the girl was coming out the bathroom with the kit and towels and saw Jesse leaving, she screamed, Jesse please don't go, I'm going to make everything all right. Fuck that Jesse said, this will be the last time you see my black ass. Jesse went down the steps three at a time leaped in his car and got rubber getting out of there; and call another old girl he knew. Hello Doris you won't believe what just happened to me, I was on my way to Mickey D's for some breakfast for us because I know you work late and all, and I just wanted to do something nice for you.

Yeah Jesse, and?

When I was getting in my car two old boys jump me. One stab me in my back pretty good, if I wasn't as fast as I was he would have had me down for the count. I need you Doris, I'm hurt.

Jesse you lucky I'm a nurse or you'll have to take your ass right to the clinic. Come on over, and Jesse, you aren't getting any.

Baby, I'm bleeding like a stuff pig, and I'm about to fallout here. Blood getting on my car seats, Draws? That's the last thing on my mind.

After Jesse hung up he said to himself, that's what she always say. Five minutes later the phone rang and Jesse said it's eight in the morning who would be up at this time of morning except that crazy bitch I just left. Yeah, Jesse said.

Jesse this is Willow, got a minute?

Well I'll be damned never figured I ever hear from you again. What do I owe the pleasure of this call?

I'll cut to it Jesse, I know you not for no bullshit, I need your help.

You or the agency, Jesse said?

One and the same, you know they got me by the balls, if I had balls.

Willow, I just can't do it, the last time we were together I got my ass shot off and my ankle in a cast, and I think I could have had a future with Seaman's. They were where it's at.

Yeah, Willow said but where are they today?

Good point Jesse said. Never the less I'm tied up, busy, busy, and busy. You wouldn't believe all the things I'm into.

Stop it Jesse, you know the agency been watching you even if they did give you that pardon. Besides, all you're doing is screwing yourself to death and running from woman to woman.

Damn Willow, why you so hard on me? A guy's got to live.

Look I've contact Malone and she's in and this may be the tiebreaker for you. You may get a chance to see Samantha again.

Jesse immediately pulled over to the side of the road and stop the car. What did you just say?

Samantha, she'll be on this Op somewhere down the line.

How far down the line? Jesse said.

I can't tell you that Jesse but she'll be there.

You not bullshiting me are you Willow?

No way Jesse, she'll be there.

In that case I'm in, Jesse said. Where and when?

Six months ago almost to the day he was lying in bed with Samantha both stark-naked. She was the finest woman Jesse had ever laid eyes on, much less make love to. They made love often from eight that night till noon the next day. Jesse was never one to go to sleep on a good lay and it seems like nether was she. They made love, talked very little, drank champagne, made love and made love some more. There was a tray of food next to the bed but was never touched. What a night!

Jesse had met Samantha on that last operation he was on, after the feds bullshit him into it. Well he really didn't have a choice it was either that or go to jail for a long period of time. There were two other women with me bout in the same situation, Dorothy Malone and Janice Willow. We had to bust this high roller, he had setups in about three different countries, drugs, white slavery, prostitution, murderous, kid's pornography. That really hit me the hardest. Samantha had penetrated their operation with a partner who got caught and killed. Willow, Malone and I managed to get inside kill the top people and put a halt to some of their operation. I hear they have a new boss now and back in business. They were going to sale Samantha to the Saudis for the highest bidder, turn out she sold for a cool $1 million. When we got there I was the one that saved her you might say but in reality she saved me. But she felt it was me and wanted to show her appreciation. And she did, again, again and again.

Dorothy Was at pool side talking to a young man 10 years her junior she had met him the night before, myty in her hand, wearing a swimsuit that was really much to revealing. But she could get away with it, what the hell she thought, if you got it, FLANT it. At 5 foot 11 and 132 pounds and 42 years old, she had even lost pounds thanks to a job she taken with the FEDS. That was some two weeks +6 months of training. But things worked out. We finish the job, the FED'S gave me my pardon and a nice little allotment along with it. If I watch my finances I should be good for some years to come, and now I'm here in the Bahamas and loving it. That is until I received a call from

Janice Willow. If Janice call then I know it's for the agency, they got some kind of hold on her and are not going to let go. I received my pardon for a job I did for them with the help of Willow and Jesse, but when offered a job I put them on hold. That was six months ago since then they have not pushed me but I'll bet that's because they haven't needed me. Willow wouldn't tell me anything about the job only that she was calling Jesse also. Well I guess I should try to get back to work, I'm not getting any younger and the FEDS do pay well. At least this time I won't be doing it for my freedom but for Lincoln, Jackson and Hamilton. It'll be good to see Jesse again he turn out to be an A-Okay

little guy, just stays Horney all the time. I was
wondering why all those girls seem to be running
after him and I got a chance to see for myself,
when I visited him in the hospital. I happen to
catch him coming from the bathroom in one of
those hospital gown, there supposed to fit where
they tie in the rear but he had his opened in the
front and I saw his penis. For a small man he had
the largest penis I think I ever saw. Even on men
twice his size he could give some of that to
somebody else and still have his fair share. I think
Jesse might be runt. It's a wonder he can walk
with that thing between his legs. I'd never let him
touch me with that rod, but then again you know

what they say. Never say never!

Agents Jenkins and stone

Well Sir, I didn't think we'd be calling those three back together so soon, they did do a great job on that last OP as good as our own agents. Together they make a good team, Jesse and Malone are not on our payroll yet, and do you think Willow can pull them in agent stone asked? I'm sure of it Jenkins said. We need to get ready for them, where are they located? Jesse is in Houston Texas, fifth ward, the same place he was when we picked him up about a year ago. I guess he really was home sick. Dorothy Malone is in the Bahamas, I think she'll come back with no problem, she seems to enjoy the action. Jesse, now that's another story. Well, I have confidence in Willow to have him see the light. By the way where is Willow? Jenkins asked. Believe it or not Alaska, stone said. Don't ask how she went from Australia to Germany to Alaska. Figure that one out. This next OP will bring her more to the real world I think she's used to. We did give her a short break, that last one she went on took her a week. And we don't know what she's doing on the side. She seems content, seems to like moving around. This job was made for her, if we wasn't here I think she would do it for nothing. Except for the finances, this is her world.

Willow

Alaska is no place for a woman like me to damn cold and the men are to Horney. I don't mind a few men gloating over me but damn these guys are like a bunch of Dogs, I know there short of women up here but damn. There was one local fellow caught my eye and I let him get to me. This guy talking the same bull all men talk, but then that old feeling came over me. I think I'm going to hurt me somebody, then she looked in her suitor's eyes and thought, it may as well be you. She did have the pleasure of laying up with him before killing him, If you want to call it that. After all she hadn't laid with anyone in a while now, man or woman. But since she decided to leave Alaska, she'll do this on her last night. Four days of this place is enough. The guy was really a disappointment, talk all that shit and can't deliver. I should have killed him just for that. What kind of man goes to sleep in the middle of sex anyway, that's just rude. Well he won't have that to worry about anymore and he show-nuff won't disappoint another woman. Willow received a call on her cell the next day, it was agent stone.

How you liken Alaska Janice?

Not worth a damn agent stone, I'm on my way out of here as we speak.

Tell you what Janice grab a taxi for Elmendorf Air Force Base and head for the flight line, there is a plane waiting for you.

There is something we like to discuss with you.

They'll be expecting you.

CHAPTER 2

Savanna Georgia

Royal hotel, Willow, Dorothy and Jesse met in suite 742. One thing about the feds they always travel first class, said Jesse.

They should said Dorothy, it's not their money, and it's the people's money.

I don't give a damn whose money it is as long as I can get a piece of it.

You two ready to get down to business Willow said.

She had boarded the plane at Elmendorf and while in the air was told of her assignment by agent stone. Was flown to Savanna Georgia and met up with Malone and Jesse.

Here it is, Willow said.

Bip & CY had been waiting outside the apartment for approximately 4 ½ hours now. 11 P.M., They were about to give it up but THEY Knew that time was short, they had to take care of this job within the next 24 hours. Thompson and his wife his two kids and that time limit was to make a point. Bip & CY were going to make big money for this hit, and total a half million dollars. Don't know why these people are so important but they felt it wasn't there business, money that was the only thing they were interested in. They got the right two for this job. This will make their 17th hit together, a few were made individually but together they made a good team. Hits all over the country and now savanna Georgia. A few more of these and we'll be able to retire early. A black BMW was coming down the block and up to the gate of the underground parking garage. CY checked out the license plate, XBE – 486, New York State. That's it CY said to Bip, Showtime!

After the gate open the BMW rolls into the basement garage. CY and Bip exit there rented green ford Taurus, walk across the street and entered the gate before it close. They both were holding a 22 automatic pistol with the silencer (the hit man's choice) and headed for the BMW. Outside the vehicle on each side they waited for the doors to open and then they would start firing. At that moment both men were hit with three slugs each from a 22 automatic pistol, with the silencer. Behind which were Janice Willow and Dorothy Malone, each were wearing all-black attire, CY and Bip each took two rounds in the back and one round in the head. Jesse was at the car window and told Thompson to leave and come back in an hour.

Back at the apartment and after they had gotten rid of the bodies Jesse asked, just how in the hell did we get in the BABY SITTING business?

Jesse I told you once, these people got involved with some money laundering types and kind of dealt some of money for himself. Also had a double set of books. Once his boss found out what was going down he decided to put a hit on Thompson and his family. Thompson decided to run to the Feds. But before he tells the feds anything he wants assurances from them. New identities for his self and family and all of the cash he stole from his ex-boss.

Meanwhile you got some dud in charge of the organization that don't give a damn about none of that, he just won't them dead. Thinks that will convey a message to others Jesse said.

Well the head of that organization sounds kind of dumb to me. Dorothy Said.

Look at This Jesse Said. His family, wife and seven-year-old boy and nine-year-old daughter. Thompson doesn't seem to be thinking about them very much. And another thing, that Damn BMW. Why did he have to drive that thing all the way down here from New York? If he love that thing so much why not purchased another one down here. He stole enough money!

I have no idea, that's not our worry. We were told just to look after them until all this get straightened out. He got so many hits out on him agent Jenkins said it will be better to keep him moving, said Willow

That's a hell of a lot of money out there on their asses, the fed's better hurry up and get there shit together, these guys are just going to keep on coming. Jesse said.

I'm afraid Jesse's right this time, somebody is bound to get lucky, Dorothy said. We need something better than what we got. How about thinking about splitting the family up?

Willow and Jesse looked at each other.

How would that work Jesse asked?

Well, one of us would take the kids, one would take the wife and the other the husband. And then we would all head for different parts of the country.

Yes, Jesse said and we could get us some throw away phones where not even the feds would know where we are.

And I guess we could stay in touch with each other with those same phones. Willow said.

I like it. Right now they know every move we make, like how could they know that we'd be in savannah of all places Willow said.

Money will buy you anything but this time even we won't know where we're going.

Next question is who gets who? And don't say Jesse getting the kids. Can you picture a black guy traveling throughout the country with two little white kids? No way!

Okay Dorothy said, I'll take the kids!

And I'll take the husband, Willow said.

I guess that leaves the wife for me Jesse said.

Now, if they all go along with it.

Janice, what are you going to tell agent Jenkins,

Dorothy asked?

Not a damn thing, maybe I'll email him later.

There is a leak somewhere, it could be there.

Mr. Morton:

Have we heard from our people in savannah yet?

No Sir, not a pep.

I wonder what's going on with them; they should have had that job taking care of by now. I hope we don't have to send someone else down there.

Mr. Morton the kind of money we have out on Thompson is a sure thing, we'll nail him.

I don't believe in sure things Bernie, you know that. What kind of money did you come up with, that he took; give it to me to the penny?

A little over 100 million, but since you won't to know down to be penny. Bernie said, 100 million, 200,048 balances. I'm thinking the 48 was a joke.

I got a joke for his ass once I catch him, I'd like to get him alive but I know he won't come that easy, he knows better. He should save a bullet for himself, his wife and his kids. Do you hear me Bernie?

Yes Sir.

Now, what is our government informant telling us, are they still in savannah?

He says he thinks so but even the feds have lost contact with them.

Maybe CY and BIP caught up to them, that's why they're not calling in Morton said.

I don't know Sir, somebody should have called in, either Thompson to the feds or CY and Bap to us. Something doesn't smell right Bernie said. If the feds put them under their protection program then we lost them for good. There gone and most of our operation, Bernie said.

Did you get us another accountant Bernie?

At that moment the phone rang and Bernie picked it up, listens for a few moments and disconnected.

Well, Morton said?

You're not going to believe this, they just found two bodies in the Bayou in Savannah Ga., and they think its CY and BIP. Each one had two rounds in the back and one in their heads.

You got to be kidding me; they were two of my best men. Morton said. An accountant *AND HIS WIFE COULDN'T HAVE TAKING THEM OUT LIKE THAT, THEY GOT HELP FROM SOMEBODY.* And *THE* feds *DON'T* kill like that. Whoever they are they could be working for us. What kinds of weapon were they using Morton ask?

I don't know but by the sound of the hit, I'd say 22 calibres. If CY and BIP are dead then the Thompsons are no longer in savannah.

Find them Bernie, no matter where they are find them!

AAAAAAAAAA....... hell, Dorothy was screaming to. The roller coaster does that to you sometime. The kids were holding on to her and she was holding on to them. Disney World was a good choice, the kids loved it and she had never been before. Once Thompson and wife understood what they were doing they were all for it. Two weeks should be more than enough time for the feds to get there shit together. They decided they'd be moving around continuously at some point Willow would get in touch with agent Jenkins and let him know what they were up to. Willow was still sure there was a leak; I don't think she even trusted Jenkins and he is the section chief.

What we are going to ride next Ms. Dorothy, Chris said. Anything you want, this is your day. Hey, there's Mickey, look and I see Goofy. Said Nora. This is going to be a great day said Chris.

Willow and Thompson were in Corpus Christi Texas having lunch at the beach marina at 2 PM in the afternoon. In early may it was still cool enough to sit outside on patio chairs under the umbrellas. Willow was dining on shrimp and lobster salad and tea for a side drink. Thompson had a large lobster, shrimp cocktail and Tea. They both were enjoying their lunch and eyeing the water off the coast line.

This was a hell of a change from Alaska with its cool climate even in the so-called summer. Straw hat loosely fit that cover and shaded her eyes. Her white and blue cotton dress right at her knees and sandals, no bra but panties that were more of a G-string. She felt cool for that type of climate and she loved it.

Thompson was wearing white shorts and flower sport shirt open at the collar and three fourths sleeves, beige sandals with no socks and a straw hat Louisiana style. At 5 feet 10 and 205 pounds Thompson wasn't a half bad looking guy, a little overweight but not bad. He was still almost an inch shorter than her 5 feet 11 but then a lot of men were. If she wore heels that would put her right at 6 feet.

The long slim legs and small waist with somewhat large upper chest made her look more like an Amazon and worth more than a second look. She had recently cut her hair to where it look boyish, adding to the Amazon look. From time to time Thompson would cut his eyes at her thinking" I sure wouldn't mind",

Where are Sophie and the kids Thompson asked?

I don't think you should know that in case for some reason you get compromise and what you don't know you can't tell. Safer for everyone Willow said.

Well tell me this then, when are you going to contact them to see how they are, Thompson said.

If there were any problems the team would have contacted me but it has been close to a week now so I'll give them a call later on today. I need to check in to agent Jenkins too, He's probably biting his nails about now.

Willow, is that your first name or last, Thompson asked.

It's my last name, Janice is my first. Call me Janice. And what is your first name Mr. Thompson? Willow asked

Cecil, you can call me Cecil.

Jesse:

Long Beach California. Now this is nice Jesse felt, for once Willow came through. Laying on the beach under this umbrella, cooler full of beer watching the cuties walk by, I could get use to this. Mrs. Thompson (Sophie) lying next to me and not looking half bad in her red bikini. If she wasn't hooked up to old man Thompson I would try my luck, but looking around the beach I won't need to do that.

There are some lovely ladies on the beach today wouldn't you say Jesse?

I really hadn't notice Sophie I've been kind of in my own world.

What are you thinking about Sophie asked?

Oh about being on a yacht going overseas and what it would be like, he lied. While watching another beauty pass. This is the longest I been in a long time without getting any drawls, I'm going to have to do something about that.

Jesse, Jesse? Did you hear me?

No, I'm sorry Sophie, I'm out there on that water.

You're strange Jesse, most men would be watching the girls and wishing they could go to bed with them.

Not me, I just don't go to bed with any woman, she has to be special to me. I don't care what she looks like, he lied again. "If they have a vagina he's in their".

Well I'll say Jesse, you're one in a million. I don't run across many men like you.

I'm going to hell for all this lying

I'm doing, I'm sure of it, Jesse thought.

Agent Jenkins this is Willow...

Willow, where the hell are you? Where is Thompson and his family? Why haven't you reported in? This is no good Willow, no good at all.

If you let me get a word in Willow said I'll explain all those things to you.

First of all everyone is okay, second the incident in savannah Georgia shouldn't have happened. There is a leak somewhere and I think it's on your end.

Now Willow...Jenkins said.

listen Willow said, you gave me this assignment and I'm thinking you're wanting us to carry it out and we will but to do that we have to stay alive, and in doing so keeping' the Thompson alive.

Now Willow...Jenkins said.

Here's what we're doing... Each one of us took one third of the Thompson family, Jesse has the wife, Dorothy has the kids and I have the husband. We're all in different areas of the country. We don't even know where the other is located. We all have throwaway phones so we can stay in touch with each other. I hope that explain everything for you. Now, you tell me where will you need the family and when?

Mr. Morton, contact was just made to the feds a few hours ago, we should know Thompson's location very soon now, Bernie said. We've got him now!

We'll see Bernie, we'll see! Have we got people ready to go?

Yes sir, at least two teams and one female. She's new to the organization and getting her a pretty good reputation Bernie said.

I don't give a damn if their kids as long as they could do the job. Bernie I won't the bounty raised to $2 million, I want everyone to know I really want these people.

Sir you know if we kill Thompson and his family there is no way of getting that money back.

Yeah, I've been thinking about that Bernie. Maybe we should go at this another way, let's used his kids and wife against him to get that money, then killed them.

What are the columbines saying about losing their money Bernie asked?

As you would have guess they're not very happy at all and the money is going to have to come from someone, either Thompson or myself. I've got it but I'll be damned if I am cutting it loose, so Bernie you find Thompson and the money then you kill them, in that order. Gotdamn Bernie if things don't go right we'll have to start running like Thompson.

Tell me more about this hit woman you found?

Well, she is a little different, she's Jewish, she seems to have started late in life, she is about 58 years old and used to be a history teacher. Unmarried, no kids. She has about five kills to her credit and her weapon of choice is the 22 and is very good with it as you can see by the kills she had. She is known as the teacher. She wears those black horn rimmed glasses, bow in the rear of her hair that's rolled into a bun. White silk blouse with ruffles, black Ike jacket and skirt down to her ankles. Old grandma shoes with those Hugh heels. You get the picture. She'll fool the hell out of you. Then before you know it, Bam!

Agent Stone walked into Jenkins office, yes sir?

I've heard from Willow, she seems to be taking over this operation. She also seems to think that there's a mole at our end.

I don't know sir, you know Willow seems to have a nose for those kinds of things that's one of the reasons we wanted her. And it wasn't any accident those hit boys showed up in savannah, that was supposed to be hush-hush. We found out about the hit just in the nick of time Stone said so if willow's right where could it have come from? We're the ones who are supposed to be doing the eavesdropping, we're working with the NSA, the CIA and we're the FBI. What the hell is going on? Tell you what agent Stone start an inquiry into who is leaking and where it's coming from but you know you will have to be doing it on the Q.T...

Yes sir I know, I'll take care of it.

The teacher was at an outdoor café in San Francisco California having an iced tea at 2 PM in the afternoon, umbrella open 10 or 20 customers doing the same thing. Some had a light lunch with a beer or margarita on the side discussion the day's events and what the coming night will bring. The teacher wasn't interested in nothing they had to say but had her eyes on one somebody, that one somebody was a 23-year-old student at the local university. 5 foot four, hundred and 25 pounds heavenly suntanned very nice shape. Hair boyish style, shorts and tank top. No bra looked like, probably no panties either. Typical young girl. Today she would die!

She made one mistake, being the mistress of a man who wife did not play that and who was willing to pay big bucks to make her go away. With half being paid the girl was already as good as dead. The girl in question had been sitting at the table about 45 minutes with two other girls doing what young girl do. Shooting off at the mouth, talking on that damn cell phone even when they're talking to each other at the table. I can't stand those damn things. It's about time somebody went to the ladies room, that'll be my chance then if they all don't go together.

Three days is enough time spent on this young lady, I need to move on to the next job. Teachers cell phone rang she glanced at the viewer and noticed it was her recruiter. Yes, she said.

Are you free?

Soon!

As soon as you are there is a six figure payday waiting for you that I think you'll like.

Is that right!

Yes, so let me know as soon as you're free.

I certainly will.

At this time the student and one of her friends stood up and were headed toward the ladies room, the friend that was left at the table call one of the girls back to the table as she held up her cell phone. The student that the teacher was stocking continued on to the ladies room.

The teacher stood up and followed her. In the ladies room no one was visible so the teacher started looking underneath the stall doors. Out of the four stalls there was one that was occupied, number three. The teacher took out her 22 with the silencer, fired three times through the door at the level she thought the girl would be. Put the weapon back in her purse and walked out.

CHAPTER 3

Hello Willow, agent Jenkins here. I just wanted to let you know what was going on.

I'm glad you got things together it's been close to two weeks now Willow said. How soon will they be leaving?

About another week we'll have everything in place, how is everything going on your in?

Thompson and I are good and the others are hanging in there also, we're just waiting on you.

Give us another week I'll call you and you can call the others Jenkins said.

A few days' later Willow and Cecil were walking in the old section of Corpus Christi sightseeing in the store windows. When they came upon an old antique store. There were paintings, furniture and jewellery. While looking at the display Willow saw a ring that called her, it had her hypnotized. Cecil noticed her and look to see what she was looking at. What are you looking at he said?

Willow didn't speak at first then she said, that ring there.

Are you talking about the Opel?

No, Willow said, the one next to it.

Cecil looked closer and pointed to the one he felt it was. That one, the Medusa?

Yes, the Medusa!

Why would you want something that hideous? Cecil said?

I don't know it's just something about it that I like and I want it, and I'm going to get it.

Besides, that medusa will match the one she has tattoo on her butt.

The ring was Ebony in color, it had the face of the Gorgon with eyes made of emeralds. Snakes for hair and ruby's on each side.

Let me get it for you Cecil said.

You don't have to do that Willow said.

I want to Cecil said, let me do that for you. All you and the team are doing for me and my family.

So Willow and Cecil went inside the shop to purchase the ring.

The clerk informed them that particular ring had been in the shop forever, they couldn't get rid of it.

You've gotten rid of it now Willow said and proceeded to put it on.

The ring went on her left index finger like it was meant to be there. She kissed Cecil on his cheek and said, how can I ever thank you!

I'm sure we'll think of something Cecil said.

When Willow and Cecil return to the yacht where they were staying there were two visitors waiting for them, mud and Jeff. A.k.a.... Heavy and little bear. Heavy was 360 pounds, 6 feet five, square features and pug nose. Hitler type moustache with a bald head. Jeff was a Blackfoot Indian, 5 foot five, hundred and 50 pounds sporting a ponytail.

As Cecil and Willow walked in the cabin Heavy was there sitting at the table drinking a glass of wine and smiling, Holding a Glock 30s loosely in his hand. Coming up behind them was Jeff holding a Smith and Wesson MP9.

Glad you two could join us we got a lot to talk about, heavy said.

First things first, where is the money? Heavy asked.

How did you find us Willow asked?

You don't get to ask the questions here so shut the fuck up, heavy said.

So, Ms. Lady sit your ass over on the bed and let us talk to Mr. Thompson.

By the way Jeff, pat the good people down, we don't want any surprises. Heavy **said.**

Cecil stood in the middle of the cabin when Jeff went over and started patting him down, when finish he went over to Willow to where she was sitting on the bed. He looked down at her breasts and said "girl you show got something on you" damn! Hey heavy how about me knocking this out before we get started?

Not on your life, business first then pleasure, heavy said.

Jeff told Willow to stand up, and started patting her down starting at the breasts (he had to reach up) to the hips and up her skirt. With a longer pat on her butt. Her purse carried a Beretta with two clips.

And what are we going to do with this Jeff asked?

There are snakes out and about you can't be too careful, Willow said.

Now Thompson, to save time why don't you just tell us where the money is and we can be on our way, still friends.

I'm sure if Mr. Thompson knew where the money was he would tell you Willow said.

Shut up bitch you talking too much, heavy said. We want to hear from Thompson and he better start talking soon.

Jeff, help Mr. Thompson out!

Jeff turned around and hit Cecil upside his head with his gun, Cecil drop to the floor on one knee and grab the side of his face. His left eye started to swell and close.

At that moment Willow reached behind her back where she kept her Chinese throwing knife hidden (whish Jeff had missed) and grab him by his ponytail, pulled his head back and cut his throat from ear to ear.

It happened so fast that heavy had no time to react. His pistol still hanging by its finger guard and pointed down.

Cecil grab the weapon away from heavy and Willow throw her knife into heavy's collar bone.

Got damn! Got damn! What the fuck just happen heavy said. Grabbing his left collarbone trying to stop the bleeding.

Willow stepped over Jeff's body and picked up her weapon and his. She told Cecil to hold on to heavy's weapon.

Got damn, got damn! Heavy Repeated. I need a doctor, I need a doctor!

Shut the hell up, for a big man you sure whine a lot.

What'll we do now, Cecil asked.

After you help me do something then you head for stash house number two and I'll meet you there, take a cab and leave the rental car. Take my bag and put it in the car before you go.

After Cecil had left heavy being tied with duct tape, his hands behind him and his legs together. All accept his mouth.

Willow sat down across from him with a glass of wine and crossed her legs. She had taken her knife out of Heavy's collarbone and in doing so she twisted it a time or two, making sure it bleed as much as possible. She sipped her wine and just looked at him.

What do they call you? Willow asked.

Heavy, they call me Heavy.

Are you just going to let Jeff lay there? Aren't you going to cover him up or something? Don't leave him like that.

He'll be okay; I don't believe he's hurting any Willow said. You need to worry about Heavy.

Who sent you? Willow asked.

I don't know heavy said, we just get a phone call and are told who and where. Are you going to kill me?

Where did the call come from?

New York I think I'm not sure; could you stop the bleeding in my shoulder?

What is the person's name in New York?

Hell, I don't know; I heard something like Marvin, Melvin, Martin or Morton something like that.

You are telling me the truth aren't you, Willow said.

I am, I am, I have no reason to lie. You got me over a barrel. And you are going to let me go so I am grateful for that.

Willow stood up after finishing her wine and told heavy "don't go nowhere, I'll be right back".

Up on deck she started the yacht and headed for the Gulf of Mexico.

After departing the Marina and out in the open sea area she went back below deck and collected heavy.

Back up on deck she told Heavy this is where we part company.

What are you talking about, I've told you all I know. You are going to let me go aren't you?

Sure, I'm not like you. I know what you had in store for me and Cecil. But no I'm not going to kill you but I do need time to get away and this is the only way I know. Now get into the raff it should take you a few hours to get yourself loose and get back to shore.

That damn rubber raff is not going to whole me and you know it, heavy said.

You better hope it does, Willow said. That's the best you goanna get.

After getting into the raff with willow's help heavy said, yeah; this should work.

I'm glad Willow said and released the line that was attached to the yacht and let it drift away, after the raff was 20 feet away she pulled her weapon and put three holes in it.

The sharks goanna eat well tonight she said to heavy!

Hey! Hey! Hey bitch. What the fuck are you doing?

You lying bitch, you mother fucker, your mama is a mother fucker, your daddy is a mother fucker, your mama, and mama is a... At that moment water was up to heavy's ankles and then to his knees. Because of his weight he was going down fast. And then he screamed. I – can't – swim. You know good m.f.... bitch.

Willow had pulled further away from the raff at this point and was thinking about dumping Jeff's body further out to sea and to find out how in the hell they were located.

Chapter 4

Agent stone stepped in agent Jenkins office and said, yes Sir?

I received a call from Willow she informed me they were attacked by two men. Their names were heavy and Jeff, heavy is a 360 pound white man and Jeff is an Indian.

Were, as in past tense, agent stone asked?

She says that she took care of it and the men won't be seen again. She wants to know how they found them and so do I, Jenkins said.

Stone said we're working on the assumption that there is a leak and by the attack it looks like there may be. We are putting something together now but it may take a while to work it out but I'm sure we'll work it out.

Well I hope so if not their go's I'll case along with one dead family and possibly three dead agents, Jenkins said. You got any idea where those leaks are coming from Jenkins asked?

Some but you may not like what I have in mind,

I'd like to keep it to myself for now stone said.

Well don't keep it too long I got a feeling we're

running out of time.

What a about the others Sir, are they okay?

So far, so good. Willow is contacting Jesse and

Dorothy to let them know about the attempted hit.

So you don't call Jesse and Dorothy is that right,

you only call Willow. Stone asked?

Yes that's right, what are you getting at Jenkins asked?

If you don't mind I'd like to hold on to what I'm thinking till I know for sure. But you may not like what I come up with.

Damn that Jenkins said, let the chips fall where they may we must find that leak and quick.

Jesse and Susie were staying near the beach in a 250 condo complex, the apartments were set in a number three form with the front in some area facing the back and others. The apartment numbers were in Roman numerals. To find your apartment you would need your card key and once near it your door would automatically unlock. The back sliding door had no number on it so you had to pretty much know where your apartment was. There was a pool in the front and a pool in the rear, there were three pools in all. Jesse walked into the apartment and told Sophie that he'd been walking around for 15 minutes trying to find the apartment. How in the hell do anyone find their way around here it's like a damn maze, Jesse said.

Well, on the other hand if it's that hard for us to find ourselves around just think how hard it'll be for the ones that are searching for us, Sophie said. Plus there is a map on the inside closet wall.

I guess you're right but I'm glad Willow gave us a heads up about her situation and to be on alert.

Did Willow go into detail about what happened to them Sophie asked? Did anyone get hurt? How is Cecil?

Willow is never going to tell you everything just that they were attacked and they are okay Jesse said. Knowing Willow that means the attackers are not okay.

You play poker, Jesse asked?

No, but I do play other games!

Later on that night Mr. and Mrs. Brown, a.k.a. Salt and pepper. Were sitting inside their rental Toyota four Runner drinking a cup of coffee.

What time do you think we should hit them Mrs. Brown (pepper) asked?

It's about 2:30 AM now I would say three would be a good time Mr. Brown said. Remember Thompson's wife must not be harmed but the person who's with her is history Mr. Brown said. Did you check out their apartment?

Yes, Mrs. Brown said. I'll go in through the back, off him and take Mrs. Thompson hostage and bring her out to the car.

You sure you don't want me to take this one, Mr. Brown asked?

No, Mrs. Brown said, no sense changing a winning combination. It's worked well for us many times before

The Browns were wearing their work attire which was black slacks, silk pulled over Blouse for her and a T-shirt for him. Silk jacket for both and a fedora. Black Socks and loafers with rubber soles.

The weapon of choice were the switchblade and P 22 with silencer. Mr. Brown carried a backup on his left ankle.

Did you make sure everything was turned off at the house, the garage door down, the coffee pot and TV, security alarm? You know how you forget, Pepper said.

I'm sure (I think) I'll double check it right now and grabbed his cell phone and commence to check all the things his wife had mentioned.

It's time, pepper said.

Bernie, have we gotten word from I'll two men in Corpus Christi Texas yet? Morton asked.

Not a word, it's like they disappeared off the face of the earth, I get this feeling they been taken out. They would have called in by now Bernie said.

And the other team we sent out Morton asked? What are their names? Salt and pepper, a husband and wife team. They've been out there together five years or more working for us but not a word from them either.

What the fucks going on Bernie? All our people are going in but they're not coming out.

Morton's phone rang, he listened for a few minutes and hung up.

What's up Bernie's asked?

The Browns are both dead. The wife it seems tried to enter the wrong condo occupied by a cop and his wife, they had just been out celebrating their anniversary.

They were just about to have sex when pepper tried to come in through the patio door. She got one shot off when the cop put three in her chest.

Mr. Brown heard all the commotion and knew something was wrong and tried to make a run for it, and in doing so he ran right smack into a police car and two cops. He tried to shot it out with them, he didn't make it.

Damn Bernie said. Ever since this thing began it's been nothing but bad luck, what the hell are we going to do now?

The kids, Morton said. We have to go after the kids. Once we connect with them we'll have Thompson by the balls. Locate the kids for me Bernie, locate the kids.

The teacher was told that the kids and their handler were in the Orlando Florida area and had been for close to a week. The rented house they were in was a three-bedroom two-bath, kitchen and family room. Small backyard with connecting garage.

Her instructions were not to hurt the kids (yet) but take them hostage, if the handler get in the way then take her out. After checking out the house finding it empty and putting bugs and surveillance cameras in a couple of the rooms she left to find a secure area a mile away to wait. She wouldn't wait until tonight if possible she'd hit them when she could.

Meanwhile Dorothy and the kids were at the Lake and had been for a few hours. They had a picnic basket with them and felt like they had no worries whatsoever. Willow had gotten in touch with her and told her of the attempted hit on her and Thompson and they think the attempted hit on Jesse.

There is some good news, we all can come in out of the cold soon. We'll all meet in Clovers, New Mexico and the feds will take the family off our hands.

Good deal Dorothy said. We're at the lake now so we'll just finish out the day and get ready to get out of here come tomorrow.

I'll see you in clovers on Thursday then, Willow said. Be careful Dorothy.

Good news agent stone said as he entered Jenkins office we located the leak! You won't believe this, the leak originated right here in your office, off your secure line.

Tell me your lying Jenkins said.

No Sir, we traced it right from your line to Willow, from Willow to Dorothy to Jesse. But it all started when you call Willow, and guess what? One of our own people did it and they work for the NSA.

He just hooked on to your line and whenever you would call Willow he would trace it on to who Willow would call and get their location that way. It was just that easy.

So we got him the same way, whenever he picked up on your private line we picked up on him.

What all do they know now? Jenkins asked

We are debriefing him now Sir, it shouldn't be long. Stone said

7 PM Tuesday evening Dorothy and the kids return to the house.

What about a pizza kids she asked.

Yeah, we won't pizza, we won't pizza the kids echoed.

Okay, I'll order one right now. You're going to need to take your bath and by the time you do that I think the pizza will be here.

One hour later the doorbell rang and Dorothy answered the door thinking it was the pizza delivery man but a little old lady holding a large pizza in her left hand with a weapons stick underneath held by her right hand. She told Dorothy to move back "please".

Dorothy saw right away that the little lady was very serious so she immediately step back.

Where are the kids the teacher asked?

In the bathroom Dorothy said. Their finishing taking their bath.

There was a straight-backed chair in the family room, the teacher told Dorothy to sit down in it and handed her a tie wrap to secure herself to the chair handle. After her left wrist were secure she walked over behind her and placed the other tie on her right wrist.

I'm glad you're being so cooperative, I really didn't want to have to kill you so soon.

Thank you for that, Dorothy said.

The kids came out of the bathroom laughing and playing and screaming "is the pizza here yet?" We won't pizza.

Then they spotted Dorothy tied to the chair and the teacher standing over her with a weapon.

Bernie ran into Morton's office and said, we got lucky. The teacher grab the kids down in Florida, we got him now.

Well it's about time, Morton said. Now to contact him.

Willow answered the phone, hello?

Let me speak to Thompson Morton said.

Who is this Willow said.

Damn that Morton said tell him it's the person that has his kids.

Willow looked at Cecil and Cecil Saw the look on her face and asked, what is it.

Bad news Willow said and handed him the phone.

Hello, Cecil said.

Thompson, where the hell is my money?

Cecil was stunned and didn't say a word.

Cat got your tongue Thompson, I want you to know that I have your kids and I will kill them if I don't get my money.

Let my kids go Morton, they have nothing to do with this.

They have everything to do with this, it's all in the family Morton said.

Willow took the phone from Cecil, if you have the kids then let us talk to them, if you can't do that then get the hell off the phone.

I can do that, I'll get back with you Morton said.

Bernie, get a hold of the teacher and have her call us we need to let Thompson know we have the kids and that there alive.

Bernie called the teacher and she picked up on the second ring

Yes! The teacher said.

We need to let the father know the kids are alive and well Bernie said.

How do you won't to handle it? Teacher said.

Call this number, let him talk to the kids and then stand by for further instructions.

Chapter 5

Agent stone walked into Jenkins office and said we've got it, everything we think he knows.

He's been passing all that's been said on your private line between you and Willow and in turn traced her to her location to Jesse and then to Dorothy. The person he reports to is out of New York, all he knows is Bernie but then we know that Bernie works for Morton. The bad news is we think they're on to Dorothy and the kids; he states that he did pass on that information.

Do we know where Dorothy is agent stone?

Yes Sir, the Orlando area. We should have the address very soon stone said.

With Willow in Corpus Christi and Jesse in California we're their only hope. I do expect them to be killed after they get that money back Jenkins said.

Well Morton said to Thompson did you get a chance to talk to you kids?

Yes I did Thompson said, I need a little time to think about it.

What kind of got damn time, I want that money and I want it now. What if I call my people and have them send you a finger at a time, will that help you make up your mind? Morton said.

How do I know you will keep your word and let the kids go Thompson said?

You don't, you're just have to trust me, Morton said.

Willow mentioned to Thompson to stall him and tell him you'll call him back.

Thompson inform Morton that he'd call him back as soon as he called his wife to see if she was all right.

You got an hour Morton said. After that body parts start coming off.

Willow, this is Jenkins, what's your situation there?

Willow told him where they stood and about the kids. But we're so far away there's nothing we can do.

We have our people in Orlando looking for the address it shouldn't be long now Jenkins said.

Well I hope not Willow said. We have something like an hour left before Morton start acting crazy. Dorothy will just have to come through for us.

You kids shut the hell up all you been doing is whining.

Their only kids, give them a break Dorothy said.

I give them nothing, don't like kids anyway. Shut up, you hear me! Shut up!

The teacher walked over to where they were sitting on the couch and slapped both in their faces.

Dorothy tried to jump up but the tie straps held her securely to the chair and she said to the teacher that really wasn't necessary.

You can just stay quiet to, you're really not needed you know. The teacher laid her cell phone down on the end table and walked in to the kitchen to get a glass of water.

Dorothy whispered to the kids to grab her phone and to run out the door. They both looked at her and shook their heads No!.

When a look came over Dorothy's face that made them both get up snatch the phone and run toward the front door.

The teacher spotted them when they open the door and said. Hey! Hey! Come back here.

The kids were out the door in a flash and the teacher was right behind them.

An old lady chasing two kids Dorothy knew there was no chance of her catching them.

Once the teacher was out the door Dorothy threw herself on the floor trying to burst the arms of the chair holding the tie rips.

After succeeding doing that she headed toward the bed room and her weapon.

Making sure it was loaded and the safety off she headed for the front door, as she did the teacher was coming in. Without hesitation Dorothy shot her three times in the chest, walk over to her and shot her again in the head.

Another teacher has now retired, Dorothy muttered.

Janice, this is Dorothy, what time was that meeting in clovers?

New York one week later. 526 Elmore Drive, 3 PM Saturday afternoon. Gated community.

Willow, Malone and Jesse were dressed all in white in caters uniforms, Jesse was driving the truck they were in had the logo of "Dinkins best caterers in town"

Entering the gate they made it to the third house out of five, they drove on to the rear of the house where the party was set up. They started unloading the truck and taking items to the kitchen.

Once in the kitchen Willow and Malone went through to the front of the house to the stairway, up the stairs to the third floor. Knocked on the door that they were told was the rec room and was asked to come in. The room had a professional pool table, stuffed animals around the walls and a large desk over in the corner.

Morton and Bernie was playing pool in casual dress with drinks nearby and both looked up, Surprises on their faces.

You're in the wrong place I'm afraid Morton said. The party's downstairs on the patio.

No, we're in the right place said Willow and she and Malone pulled their weapon out with the silencers.

Hey, wait a minute here, just wait a minute. What's this all about? Morton said.

What the fuck you think you're doing, you think two bitches can just come in here and threaten us Bernie said.

Easy Bernie, let's see what the ladies have on their minds, Morton said.

Fine, Willow said. Here it is!

It was okay when you sent the team after Thompson and myself, you were just trying to protect what was yours. It was even okay when you went after Jesse and Thompson's wife, just business. I can understand that. But what we can't understand is you going after the kids and we can't allow that. We can never allow that Willow said

So what the hell you bitches going to do, kill us. You ain't got the balls Bernie said. And grab his pool club and swung it at Malone who immediately put three rounds in his chest and walked over to him and put one in his head.

Malone looked at Willow, nod and walked out the room.

Morton stood in one place shocked. Wait a minute he said there should be something I can do. $1 million, I'll pay you 1 million cash to let me live.

You're out over 100 million now and I think you'll be after the Thompson till you get your money back or the Thompsons family are dead.

No, Mr. Morton you have to die.

But the Bible says to turn the other cheek, I believe that Morton said and then he broke out running toward his desk.

Willow shot him through the back of his neck, walk up to him and found he was still alive. I know the Bible says to turn the other cheek, but I'm not the one. Morton raised his hands in defence and Willow put two rounds in his head.

Willow walked back down the stairs and through the kitchen and into the rear of the van where Malone and Jesse was waiting and departed.

Epilogue

His third day between nine and midnight Jesse laid-back in his rented BMW sighed and said to himself this has been one hell of an operation this time. Most everything fucked up and on top of that no Samantha.

The only good thing that happen is Mr. Thompson sent the girls and me a nice piece of change for us helping him. I bet Mrs. Thompson had something to do with that.

Willow assured me Samantha would be at this location in the skid row section of Los Angeles California. Don't know what the hell she's doing in this area, this is the pits.

Drunks, derelicts, and the homeless they're all here and I'm study having people come up to the car asking for money.

This is my last night here, been here two nights now. Willow said Samantha would show up between 9 and 12 PM, on one of those nights. Damn, here comes another old drunk wanting money. Get the fuck out of here man, ain't got nothing for you.

10:30 PM on the last night Jesse muttered, that damn Willow has lied to me again. Damn if he didn't want to see old girl again, then he started remembering the last time they were together. Only for less than 24 hours but what a time they had.

Theo's dudes keep eyeing my wheels, I'm thinking wrong wheels for this neighbourhood, and glad I got my piece with me.

Here comes that damn bag lady again and I'll bet she'll head over my way, this is the third night I've seen her, and this must be one of her regular routes. Every time I see her she feels I have to lay something on her. I want to tell her"hey, get a job or just stay the fuck away from me.

That floppy hat on her head, the coat that's twice her size, look like she's pregnant. The dress right out of Orphan Annie, Shoes from Gonzo the clown. The teeth, let's don't talk about the teeth.

Damn! She pisses me off just looking at her and to top it off she's pushing that damn grocery cart. Oh shit, here she comes.

Hi Mr., you think you could spare a few bucks for a poor old lady?

What happened to the change I gave you last night Jesse said?

You know how it is Mr., inflation! It's not my fault, talk to the government. Now if you don't have change, I can get you change.

I'll bet you can Jesse said. Here, take this five dollars and move on down the road, I'm waiting for someone.

Is it that important that you brush me off with a lousy five dollar bill the bag lady says?

Look lady move on, I'm busy Jesse said.

Are you sure you can't spare another five Jesse?

Jesse looked at the bag lady and said; how do you know my name? Just who the hell are you?

Don't you know me Jesse? Have I changed that much since we last met?

Jesse lean out his window and toke a long hard look at who he thought was a bag lady and said.

Samantha?

www.ingramcontent.com/pod-product-compliance
Lightning Source LLC
Chambersburg PA
CBHW060126260626
47160CB00005B/2030